AN INVITATION
TO THE BUTTERFLY BALL

AN INVITATION TO THE

BUTTERFLY BALL

A Counting Rhyme

By Jane Yolen

Illustrations by Jane Breskin Zalben

CAROLINE HOUSE

Originally published by Parents' Magazine Press and Philomel Books
Published by Caroline House
Boyds Mills Press, Inc.
A Highlights Company
910 Church Street
Honesdale, Pennsylvania 18431

Publisher Cataloging-in-Publication Data
Yolen, Jane.
An invitation to the Butterfly Ball : a counting rhyme / by Jane Yolen; illustrations by Jane Breskin Zalben.
32 p. : col. ill. ; cm.
Summary: All the invited animals, from one little mouse to ten porcupines, busily prepare to attend the Butterfly Ball.
Originally published by Parents' Magazine Press, New York.
ISBN 1-878093-61-4
[1. Counting. 2. Stories in rhyme.] I. Zalben, Jane Breskin, ill. II. Title.
[E] 1991
LC Card Number 91-70416

Distributed by St. Martin's Press
Printed in Hong Kong

for

1. little Heidi

2. little Adam

3. little Jason

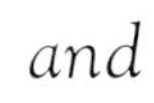

and

4. Marvin Bileck,
a big elf who is so special

AN INVITATION TO THE BUTTERFLY BALL

Knock. Knock. Who's come to call?
An invitation to the Butterfly Ball.

ONE little mouse in great distress
Looks all over for a floor-length dress.
"If I can't find one smaller than small,
Then I can't go to the Butterfly Ball."

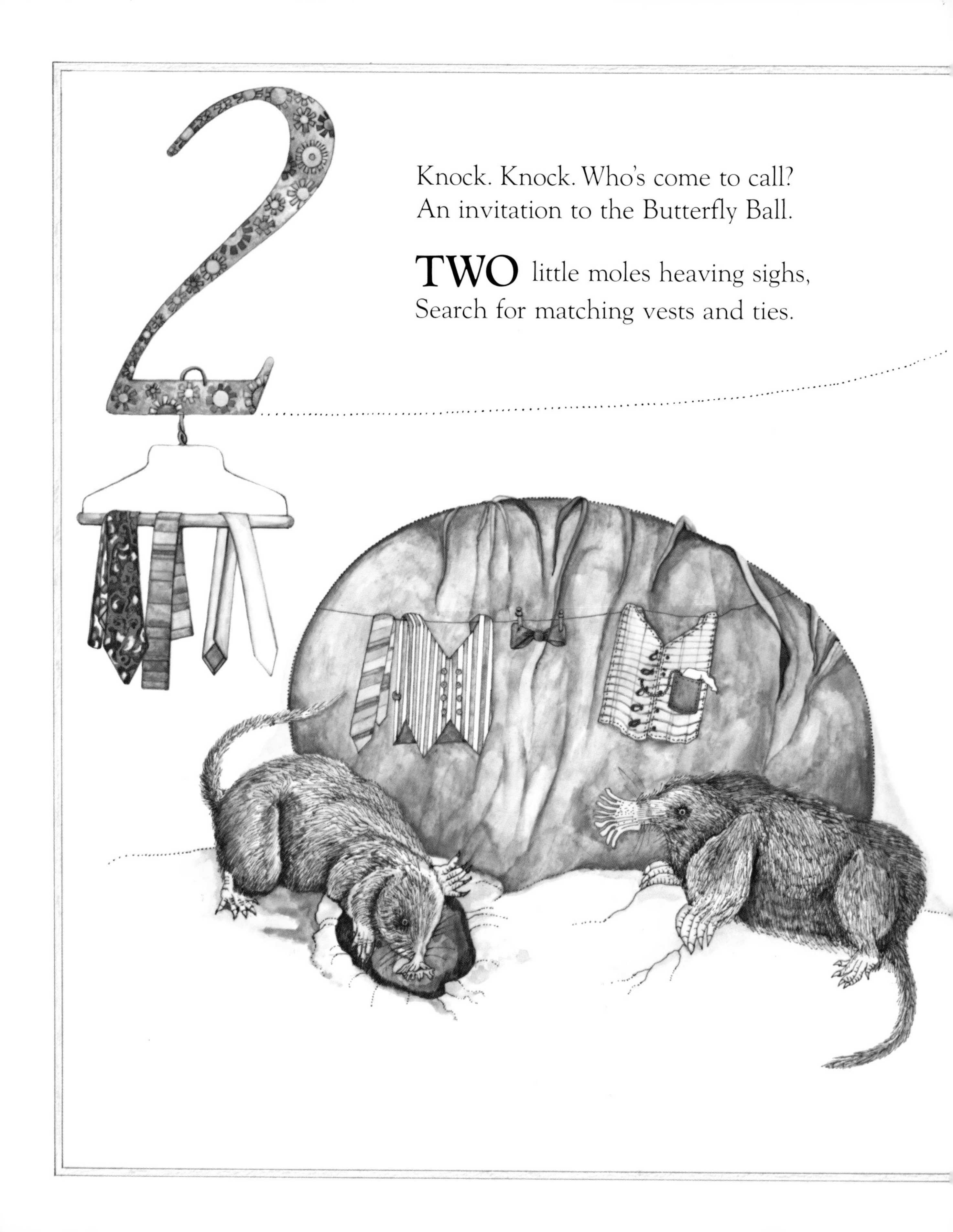

Knock. Knock. Who's come to call?
An invitation to the Butterfly Ball.

TWO little moles heaving sighs,
Search for matching vests and ties.

One little mouse in great distress
Looks all over for a floor-length dress.
If she can't find one smaller than small,
Then she can't go to the Butterfly Ball.

Knock. Knock. Who's come to call?
An invitation to the Butterfly Ball.

THREE little rabbits with very sad faces
Sort out their ribbons and baubles and laces.
Two little moles heaving sighs,
Search for matching vests and ties.

One little mouse in great distress
Looks all over for a floor-length dress.
If she can't find one smaller than small,
Then she can't go to the Butterfly Ball.

Knock. Knock. Who's come to call?
An invitation to the Butterfly Ball.

FOUR little skunks in a loud dispute,
Each one clamors for the one clean suit.
Three little rabbits with very sad faces
Sort out their ribbons and baubles and laces.
Two little moles heaving sighs,
Search for matching vests and ties.

One little mouse in great distress
Looks all over for a floor-length dress.
If she can't find one smaller than small,
Then she can't go to the Butterfly Ball.

Knock. Knock. Who's come to call?
An invitation to the Butterfly Ball.

FIVE little turtles wringing their flippers
Seek out dainty party slippers.
Four little skunks in a loud dispute,
Each one clamors for the one clean suit.
Three little rabbits with very sad faces
Sort out their ribbons and baubles and laces.
Two little moles heaving sighs,
Search for matching vests and ties.

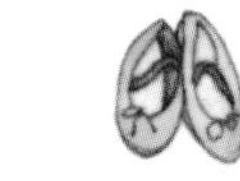

One little mouse in great distress
Looks all over for a floor-length dress.
If she can't find one smaller than small,
Then she can't go to the Butterfly Ball.

Knock. Knock. Who's come to call?
An invitation to the Butterfly Ball.

SIX little owls with mournful hoots
Long for sleek black dancing boots.
Five little turtles wringing their flippers
Seek out dainty party slippers.
Four little skunks in a loud dispute,
Each one clamors for the one clean suit.
Three little rabbits with very sad faces
Sort out their ribbons and baubles and laces.
Two little moles heaving sighs,
Search for matching vests and ties.

One little mouse in great distress
Looks all over for a floor-length dress.
If she can't find one smaller than small,
Then she can't go to the Butterfly Ball.

Knock. Knock. Who's come to call?
An invitation to the Butterfly Ball.

SEVEN little raccoons send up wails.
They cannot find their silken veils.

Six little owls with mournful hoots
Long for sleek black dancing boots.
Five little turtles wringing their flippers
Seek out dainty party slippers.
Four little skunks in a loud dispute,
Each one clamors for the one clean suit.
Three little rabbits with very sad faces
Sort out their ribbons and baubles and laces.
Two little moles heaving sighs,
Search for matching vests and ties.

One little mouse in great distress
Looks all over for a floor-length dress.
If she can't find one smaller than small,
Then she can't go to the Butterfly Ball.

Knock. Knock. Who's come to call?
An invitation to the Butterfly Ball.

EIGHT little foxes in a terrible flap,
Each one hunting for a fine wool cap.
Seven little raccoons send up wails.
They cannot find their silken veils.
Six little owls with mournful hoots
Long for sleek black dancing boots.
Five little turtles wringing their flippers
Seek out dainty party slippers.
Four little skunks in a loud dispute,
Each one clamors for the one clean suit.
Three little rabbits with very sad faces
Sort out their ribbons and baubles and laces.
Two little moles heaving sighs,
Search for matching vests and ties.

8

One little mouse in great distress
Looks all over for a floor-length dress.
If she can't find one smaller than small,
Then she can't go to the Butterfly Ball.

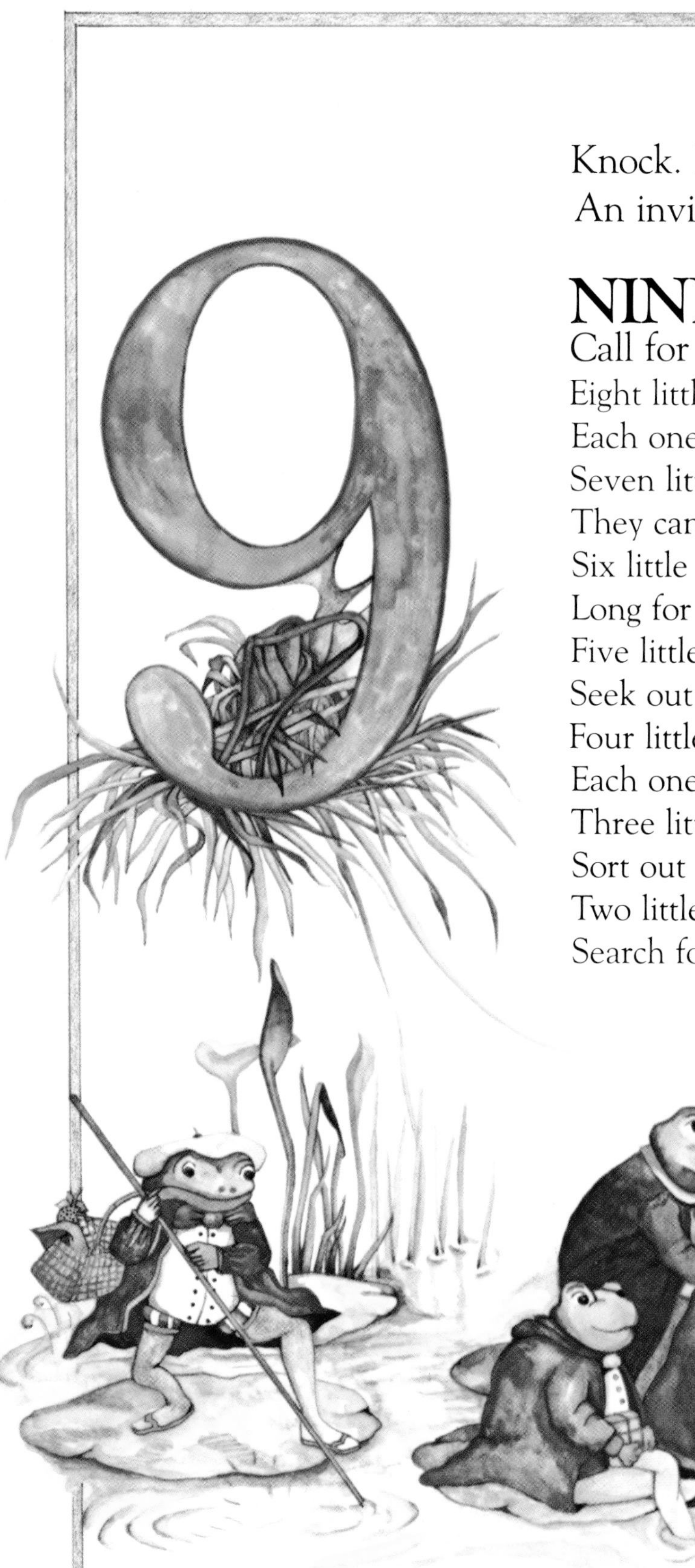

Knock. Knock. Who's come to call?
An invitation to the Butterfly Ball.

NINE little frogs with dull hoarse croaks
Call for crimson evening cloaks.
Eight little foxes in a terrible flap,
Each one hunting for a fine wool cap.
Seven little raccoons send up wails.
They cannot find their silken veils.
Six little owls with mournful hoots
Long for sleek black dancing boots.
Five little turtles wringing their flippers
Seek out dainty party slippers.
Four little skunks in a loud dispute,
Each one clamors for the one clean suit.
Three little rabbits with very sad faces
Sort out their ribbons and baubles and laces.
Two little moles heaving sighs,
Search for matching vests and ties.

One little mouse in great distress
Looks all over for a floor-length dress.
If she can't find one smaller than small,
Then she can't go to the Butterfly Ball.

Knock. Knock. Who's come to call?
An invitation to the Butterfly Ball.
TEN little porcupines set up a racket,
As they fight for the velvet evening jacket.
Nine little frogs with dull hoarse croaks
Call for crimson evening cloaks.
Eight little foxes in a terrible flap,
Each one hunting for a fine wool cap.
Seven little raccoons send up wails.
They cannot find their silken veils.
Six little owls with mournful hoots
Long for sleek black dancing boots.

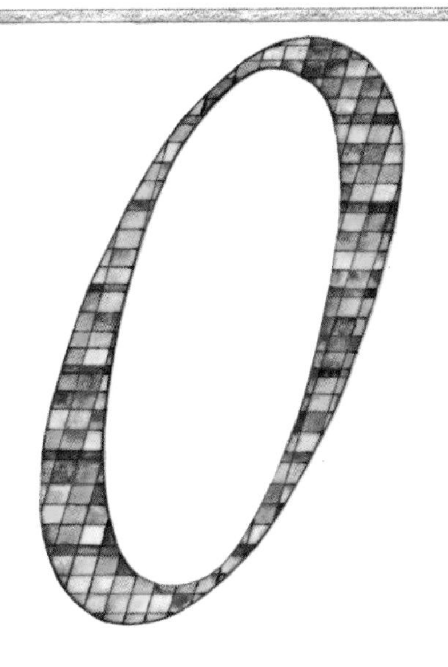

Five little turtles wringing their flippers
Seek out dainty party slippers.
Four little skunks in a loud dispute,
Each one clamors for the one clean suit.
Three little rabbits with very sad faces
Sort out their ribbons and baubles and laces.
Two little moles heaving sighs,
Search for matching vests and ties.
One little mouse in great distress
Looks all over for a floor-length dress.
If she can't find one smaller than small,
Then she can't go to the Butterfly Ball.

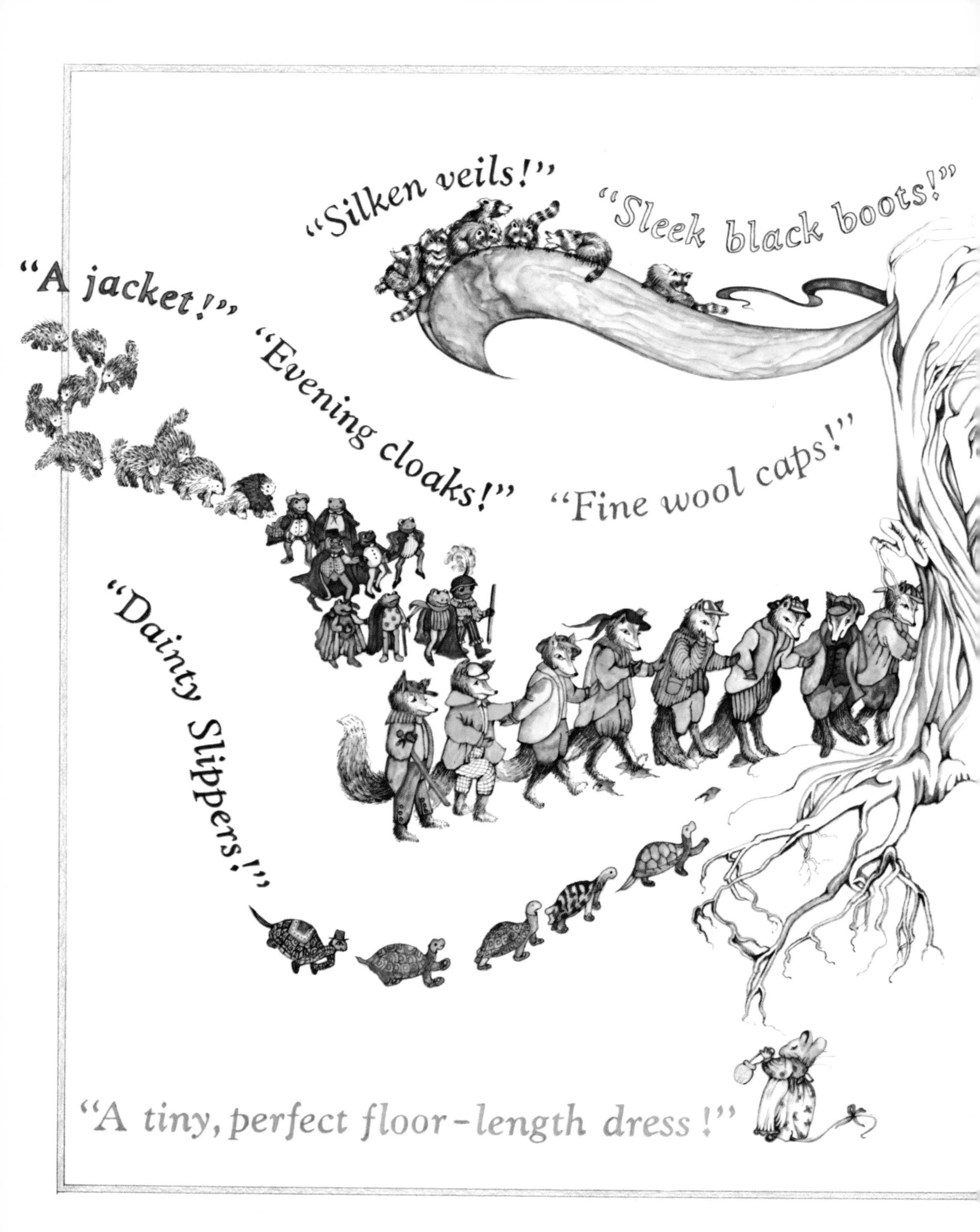
"Silken veils!"
"Sleek black boots!"
"A jacket!"
"Evening cloaks!"
"Fine wool caps!"
"Dainty Slippers!"
"A tiny, perfect floor-length dress!"

"We have found them all!
Now we can go to the Butterfly Ball."

Knock. Knock...Who's come to call?

WE HAVE!!
We've *all* come to the Butterfly Ball.

Master storyteller Jane Yolen *has written more than one hundred books for children and adults. Many of her works have won critical acclaim, including an American Library Association Notable Book for Children Award, a Lewis Carroll Shelf Award, a Golden Kite Award, and a Christopher Medal. She is the author of* Owl Moon, *the 1988 Caldecott Medal winner illustrated by John Schoenherr. She lives in Hatfield, Massachusetts.*

Jane Breskin Zalben, *a well-known writer and illustrator of children's books, is also a painter, etcher, and book designer. Among the books she has both written and illustrated are* Happy Passover, Rosie *and* Beni's First Chanukah, *a Sydney Taylor Honor Book. Her beautiful illustrations for Lewis Carroll's* Jabberwocky *have brought her particular acclaim. She lives in Port Washington, New York.*

This text was set in Goudy Old Style and the display type in Goudy Handtooled. The book was designed by Jane Zalben and Mildred Kantrowitz.